The Adventures of Goliath

Goliath's Christmas

The Adventures of Goliath

Goliath's Christmas

Terrance Dicks
Illustrated by
Valerie Littlewood

SCHOLASTIC INC.
New York Toronto London Auckland Sydney

ISBN 0-590-46593-7

Text copyright © 1986 by Terrance Dicks. Illustrations copyright © 1986 by Valerie Littlewood. All rights reserved. Published by Scholastic Inc., 730 Broadway, New York, NY 10003, by arrangement with Barron's Educational Series, Inc.

12 11 10 9 8 7   3 4 5 6 7/9

Printed in the U.S.A.   28

First Scholastic printing, December 1992

CONTENTS

Chapter One

White Christmas

It never snows for Christmas.
Everyone knows that.

Sometimes it snows before Christmas, in October or November, so that by the time Christmas comes there's nothing left.

Sometimes it snows in February or March, with Christmas far behind you and summer vacation too far ahead to even think about.

But it never snows when you want it and need it, for Christmas itself.

Well, hardly ever.

But this year it did.

David first noticed it just a few days before Christmas.

He was taking Goliath, his enormous shaggy dog, for a walk in the park.

It was a dull, gray winter afternoon, so icy cold that your breath went out in front of you in great steaming clouds.

Although it wasn't long past lunch-time, it was already getting dark, and the park looked dull and grim in the winter light.

Then, suddenly, something big and white came floating down out of the sky.

At first David thought it was a leaf.

He put out his hand, and by some miracle the white thing landed on it and clung there, icy cold and shimmering.

It was a huge snowflake.

Down came another and another until the air was filled with great cottony white lumps.

Goliath went mad with excitement, jumping up and barking and trying to

catch them, yelping with excitement
when they melted in his mouth.

Shivering with a mixture of cold and
excitement, David grabbed Goliath by
the collar, put on his leash, and dragged
him home.

They rushed into the kitchen where
David's mother was busy making
supper.

"It's snowing, Mom," yelled David. "Snowing really hard!"

His mother gave him a worried look. "I know. I hope it isn't going to affect the buses, or your dad will be late from work."

David looked at her in astonishment. He'd never understand grown-ups, he decided. How could you be worried about something as wonderful as snow?

His dad *was* late from work.

He stamped into the kitchen like a snowman, flakes of snow clinging to his overcoat and shining in his hair. "All the buses are running late," he grumbled. "Traffic's all snarled up. Honestly, you'd think we'd never had snow in this country before." He waved his evening paper, soggy with melted snow. "According to the forecast we're in for a long spell of it. Looks like we'll be having a white Christmas for once."

"Oh, they always get it wrong," said

David's mother. "It'll probably be all melted by tomorrow."

David gave her a reproachful look, but he didn't say anything.

He sneaked a quick look out of the window though. To his delight the snow was still coming down.

They spent a fairly normal evening at home, puttering around, eating supper, watching television. Every so often David would look out of the nearest window to make sure it was still snowing.

When he went to bed, later than usual because it was holiday time, he could see the snowflakes swirling around the streetlight outside his window.

When David woke up the next morning, the whole world had been transformed.

There was snow everywhere, glistening, sparkling, impossibly white snow as far as you could see.

There was a shelf of it, six inches deep, on David's window sill.

The street outside was a gleaming expanse of white—the snow was so deep you couldn't see where the sidewalk ended and the road began.

There were marks like animal tracks in the snow, left by the feet of the mailcarrier and a few early-morning travelers.

David got up, hurrying through washing and dressing and breakfast as fast as he could. He just couldn't wait to take Goliath out for his morning walk.

He had quite a job to persuade his mother to let them go. She insisted on David wearing his waterproof boots and an overcoat and scarf and a wool hat with a bobble on top. There was a last minute delay while she hunted through drawers and closets for a pair of gloves, something David never usually bothered with. She found an old pair of

gloves at last, and David, feeling at least twice his usual size, stamped down the hall, Goliath bounding ahead of him.

But when David opened the door, Goliath seemed to have a sudden change of heart. He skidded to a halt, peering suspiciously at the crispy white snow that covered the steps. He turned and gave David a reproachful look as if to say, "What is all this stuff? Is it dangerous?"

(For all his enormous size, Goliath was really a terrible coward.)

Finally David had to put on Goliath's leash and haul him out of the front door. "Come on, Goliath," he encouraged him. "It's only snow. It's fun!"

It wasn't till they reached the park that Goliath really started to enjoy the snow.

The everyday, slightly scruffy park had been transformed into a snowy plain, the pond was frozen solid, and the steep little hill looked like a sort of mini-mountain.

It was a busy scene as well as a strange one. It was obvious that David wasn't the only one pleased and excited by the snow.

Most of the families in the neighborhood seemed to be out, moms and dads and dogs, big kids and little kids.

They were playing snowballs, building snowmen, or just tramping happily through the snow like little bands of Arctic explorers on their way to the North Pole.

The hill was being used as a sled-run, with excited children whizzing down with yells of delight. Some of them had real sleds, fished no doubt from the backs of closets after years of disuse. Others had had to make do the best they could with tin trays, slabs of plywood, or anything else that was flat and big enough to sit on.

David let Goliath off his leash, made a big, round snowball, and hurled it into the distance. "Fetch, Goliath!" he yelled.

Goliath loved chasing balls and he pounded through the snow and tried to catch the snowball in his mouth as it came down.

He made a perfect catch—but the snowball, of course, disappeared . . .

Goliath gave an indignant bark, shook the snow off his nose, and came

galloping back to David, demanding another try.

David patted him on the head. "Poor old Goliath, it's not fair to play tricks on you." He fished out the well-chewed rubber ball they usually played with.

But Goliath wasn't having that. He demanded another snowball and barked till he got one.

It took several more throws to convince Goliath that snowballs just couldn't be caught, no matter how hard he tried.

David and Goliath played in the park all morning. By now Goliath was quite used to the snow and was really enjoying himself.

David remembered his dad saying that a dog of Goliath's size just had to have some St. Bernard in him somewhere.

At lunchtime they turned reluctantly towards home, making for the narrow alley that connected David's street to the park.

By now the street was looking very different from the wide band of snow David had seen in the morning. Cars had churned up a slushy channel down the middle of the road, and a city truck was out, spreading salt and sand.

There was a path down the center of the sidewalks, too, tramped out by the feet of the passersby, who had pounded the loose snow into a hard, slippery path.

Here and there people were out with shovels, clearing away the snow from their steps and the bit of sidewalk in front of their houses.

It was all very exciting and different. David made his way cautiously down the slippery street, determined to get lunch over quickly and get back out to the park.

He was just wondering what he could find to use as a sled when he heard a voice that seemed to come from nowhere.

"Help!" it called feebly. "Please, somebody help me . . ."

Chapter Two

Snowbound

David looked around in astonishment.

There was nobody near him, and there just didn't seem to be anywhere the voice could have come from.

For a moment David wondered if he'd imagined it. Then the voice came again. "Help! Please, help!"

It seemed to be coming from somewhere above his head . . .

David looked up, puzzled, but there was no one there.

He turned to Goliath, who was standing listening too, head cocked alertly.

"Find, Goliath!" said David urgently. "Where's it coming from? Find!"

"Help!" called the voice again.

Goliath woofed and dashed up the steps of the house they'd just passed. They were very steep steps piled high with snow. Goliath churned through it like a speedboat cutting through waves.

David followed after him, climbing the steps to the porch of the big old house. This house stood just in the curve of the street, and it must have been facing directly into the heart of last night's snowstorm. A huge snowdrift had piled up, almost filling the porch and covering the lower half of the house's front door.

Goliath began digging at the snowdrift, barking furiously.

Soon he'd uncovered the mail slot, and the voice came more clearly. "Help! Help!"

Someone was shouting through the mail slot! David forced his way through the snow and lifted the flap.

He saw two frightened blue eyes and caught a glimpse of white hair and gold-rimmed spectacles.

Suddenly David realized. It was Miss Gorringer, known throughout the entire neighborhood as the Cat Lady.

Miss Gorringer was crazy about cats. She kept half a dozen of them in her little apartment, and she was always leaving food out for the half-wild cats that lived in the grounds of the nearby hospital.

"It's all right, Miss Gorringer," called David. "It's David from up the street. What's the matter?"

"I'm snowed in," called Miss Gorringer feebly. "When I got up this morning I couldn't get the door open. I've been calling here for ages. The people upstairs are away for the day, and I haven't got a phone."

"Don't worry, Miss Gorringer," called David. "We'll get you out!"

He studied the front door. The first thing to do was clear the snow away.

He went down the steps and took the lid off one of the snow-covered garbage cans that stood just inside the front gate.

Banging off the crusting of snow, David went back up the steps and used the lid as a sort of scoop, clearing away the snow from the front door.

"Try now, Miss Gorringer," he shouted.

After a moment the voice called, "I still can't move it."

David frowned, studying the door. Suddenly he realized it couldn't have been the snow that was blocking the door anyway. Miss Gorringer's door, like most front doors, opened *inwards*.

David studied the edges of the door more closely and saw that they were sealed with what looked like a coating of ice. "It seems to be frozen shut," he shouted. "Stand well back and I'll see if I can get it open."

David hurled himself against the door, but since he was both small and skinny it didn't do much good.

"Come on, Goliath, you great lump, help me," he yelled.

Barking excitedly, Goliath jumped up, hitting the door with his massive front paws.

With a cracking sound the door flew open, revealing a frightened-looking Miss Gorringer sitting at the bottom of the stairs.

At the sight of David and Goliath she jumped to her feet.

"Don't you let that horrible great dog in here," she shrieked. "My cats will be terrified!"

David thought this was a bit hard on Goliath, since he'd helped with the rescue, but he said, "Stay!" to Goliath, getting a hurt look in return, and followed Miss Gorringer into her apartment.

It was an apartment full of cats, perched on chairs, cushions, and sofas.

There were six of them when you counted—one black, one white, one black and white, one tabby, one tortoiseshell,

and one ginger.

They were all enormous, like great
furry cushions, except the ginger one,
which was younger and slimmer than
the others.

"There they are," said Miss Gorringer proudly. "Bill and Ben, Sadie and Sara, Rupert, and Ginger."

At the sight of Miss Gorringer the cats all jumped down and set up a tremendous yowling, rubbing around her ankles.

"They're hungry, poor things," said Miss Gorringer sadly. "I've run out of cat food and I couldn't get out to the store."

"What about you?" said David. "Have you had anything?"

"Tea and toast," said Miss Gorringer. "That's what I live on, tea and toast. I'm all right."

David remembered his parents saying that Miss Gorringer spent all her pension money on cat food, leaving hardly enough to feed herself.

"I must get down to the store and buy some more cat food," said Miss Gorringer worriedly.

20

"I'd wrap up well," said David. "And I think I'd better come with you—it's pretty slippery out there."

He waited while Miss Gorringer put on her winter coat and boots. Then he escorted her down to the shops, making her hold his arm so she didn't slip.

Later he took her back up the street and saw her and her bag full of cat food safely back inside the house.

Goliath marched proudly beside them all the way, as if he knew David was doing an important job. When they arrived back Miss Gorringer patted him on the head. "He seems a nice enough animal, though I don't care for dogs as a rule. They chase my cats, you know."

David grinned. "Goliath doesn't chase cats, it's the other way around! I'll come back with a shovel after lunch and clear your steps and porch."

"You're a kind boy," said Miss Gorringer. She tried to give him fifty

cents, but David wouldn't take it. He was
sure she didn't really have enough
money for herself—not with all those
great big fat cats to feed.

As he was saying good bye, the ginger
cat made a determined attempt to dash
out of the front door. Miss Gorringer

tackled him just in time, grabbing him the way a football player grabs the ball.

"Come inside, you bad boy. He's younger than the others, you know, and still a bit wild!"

"Don't you ever put them out?" asked David.

"Only in the garden with me keeping an eye on them," said Miss Gorringer. "Even then I have to be sure they don't climb over the wall and end up in the park. No telling what might happen to them out there!"

David's mother was a bit cross when he came home very late for lunch, but she soon forgave him when he told her what had happened. "What a good thing you came along. She might have been stuck in there for ages."

"It was sensible of you to see her to the store," said his father. "Icy weather is very dangerous for older people. They

23

can easily fall and hurt themselves."

"That's right," said David's mother. "And Miss Gorringer isn't the only older person on this street. I'm going to call a special meeting of the Neighborhood Association. We must make sure that the older people are managing all right in this terrible snow."

"As a matter of fact," David's mother went on, "I think we ought to have some kind of special Christmas party for them."

"We could hire a room in the Fox and Hounds," said David's dad. "There's a nice room with a fireplace there, and it'd be handy for them."

"I'll talk to Miss Gorringer this afternoon," said David's mother. "She's the president of the Association, you know. If she agrees it's a good idea, we can start organizing it right away."

It seemed like a very good idea at the

time. A real Christmassy sort of idea.

But no one had any idea of all the trouble it was going to cause—especially for David and Goliath.

In fact, it nearly ruined Christmas altogether.

It happened like this . . .

Chapter Three

Missing

It was several days later that the disaster happened.

It was the Tuesday before Christmas—the day of the neighborhood party.

Money had been collected from pretty well everyone on the street, and all the neighbors were making cakes and pies and sandwiches.

Bill, the manager of the Fox and Hounds, a local restaurant, had agreed to provide a good roaring fire in his private room, and to sell them whatever they needed to drink.

David was tramping up the road, his sled on his back and Goliath on his leash. They were on their way to the park for a last bit of sledding before it got too dark.

David's sled was a big sheet of shiny plastic, and was in fact an abandoned real estate agent's sign that he had found propped up next to a trash basket.

Seeing the possibilities, David had carted it home and drilled holes in the front edge, fitting on a big loop of rope that he could jam his feet in and hold on to steer.

It was an odd-looking setup, but it was amazingly efficient, and David's homemade sled was much faster than the fancy store-bought ones owned by some of his friends.

It had become quite famous among the local kids, and David was on his way to a challenge race against a boy who owned a flashy, ultra-modern sled with gleaming steel runners that his dad had just bought him.

As he reached the top of the street he heard a voice call, "David!" He looked around and saw Miss Gorringer standing behind her door, which was open just enough for her to peep out. "Could you come here a minute, David?"

Telling Goliath to "Stay," David went up the steps. "Are you all right, Miss Gorringer?"

He had cleared all the front steps for her, so she could easily get in and out.

Miss Gorringer thrust a crumpled envelope through the crack in the door. "Would you take this down to the Fox and Hounds for me, David? I've got so much to do and I'll never be ready if I go. It's the money to pay for the party."

David hesitated, and Miss Gorringer said worriedly, "If I have to trail all the way down there and back I'll never be ready, and we promised the manager to have it for him this afternoon."

David sighed. "All right, Miss Gorringer, I'll look after it."

"Take it straight there, won't you? Mind you don't lose it on the way. I've got a cake to make and my cats to feed, and . . ."

She popped back inside, closing the door on her muttering.

David stood for a moment, looking at his watch. The trouble was that if he had

to trail all the way down to the restaurant and back up to the park, he would be late for his race and everyone would say he'd chickened out . . . He could deliver the money later.

There was a zipped pocket inside his coat, and the money would be safe enough there. Tucking the money away and zipping the pocket David set off for the park.

The race was a triumph. David's signboard sled was the winner by several yards, and Goliath galloped along behind him barking triumphantly.

Accepting the congratulations of his friends, David picked up his sled. Patting his pocket to make sure the money was still there, he set off for the restaurant.

It was closed when he got there, though the door was still open.

David went up to the bar, where a

jolly-looking girl was washing glasses.

She grinned at him cheerfully. "We're closed, sonny—and anyway, you're too young!"

"I know," said David. He produced the precious envelope. "Would you give this to the manager, please? It's the money for the Christmas party."

"Senior Citizens' bash, eh?" said the jolly girl. "I hope they don't get wild and smash the place up." She took the envelope and stuck it between two bottles behind the bar. "Dad's busy in the cellar, but I'll see he gets it as soon as he comes up."

David said thank you and made his way home.

It was just as he was finishing his afternoon snack that the trouble really started.

Their doorbell rang, his dad went to answer it, and a few minutes later David heard angry voices in the hall.

Then he heard his dad say, "He's here now. You'd better come in."

His dad came into the kitchen, bringing with him a fat, bald-headed man in a dark blue suit. "This is the manager of the Fox and Hounds, David. There seems to be some problem about the money for the Christmas party."

David jumped up, alarmed. "How can there be? I gave it to a girl behind the bar."

"That's right," said the man grimly. "She gave it to me as soon as I came out of the cellar. Here's the envelope—and here's what was in it!"

He slammed an envelope down on the table. It was open now, and sticking out of it was a wedge of paper, folded square, that looked as if it had been torn from some magazine.

David snatched up the envelope and examined it. That was all there was. Just the envelope and the folded magazine pages.

There was no sign of any money at all.

David gasped, "But that's impossible. Someone must have taken it."

"Well, it wasn't my daughter Rosie," said the fat man fiercely. "Besides, no one had time to. I came up from the cellar just a few minutes after you left, and she gave me the envelope. I opened it, and that's what I found. What's in that envelope is what you delivered."

David's father said gently, "Tell us
about it from the beginning."

David told them about passing Miss
Gorringer's house and about her giving
him the money.

Immediately the fat man pounced. "And did you bring it straight to me?"

David looked guilty. "Well, no, not exactly. You see there was this sledding race in the park, and I didn't want to be late . . ."

The manager turned to David's father. "There you are, then. Obvious, I call it. Kid takes the money to the park and loses it while he's playing. Envelope must have come open. Then he panics, stuffs some paper in, and brings it around, hoping somehow he'll get away with it."

"It wasn't like that," said David desperately.

The manager wasn't listening. "Well, I'm sorry, but you don't pay for parties with old magazines. Unless that money reaches me by opening time tonight, there won't be any party!"

He turned and marched out, and they

heard the front door slam behind him.

David's mother said reproachfully, "David, how could you be so careless?"

"I couldn't and I didn't!" yelled David. "I tell you I didn't lose it . . ."

His parents went on talking as if he weren't there. "How much was it?" asked David's father.

His mother frowned. "About a hundred dollars, I think."

"We'll have to make it good," said his father slowly. "It'll wipe out all our Christmas money, though." He looked at his watch. "Trouble is, I don't see how I can get my hands on the cash by five-thirty when the restaurant opens. The bank's closed now. . . Maybe one of the stores would cash a check."

"*You* mustn't pay it back," said David, seeing all the Christmas jollity and presents disappearing. "I didn't lose it!"

"I'd like to believe you, son," said his

father. "But how else could it have happened?"

"Maybe those restaurant people stole it."

His father shook his head. "Old Bill's a grumpy old fellow, but no one ever said he wasn't honest."

David's mother turned to him in despair.

"Then if they didn't steal it, and you didn't lose it, what did happen?"

David jumped to his feet. "I'm not sure. But I'm definitely going to find out! Come on, Goliath!"

Before anyone could stop him, David snatched up the envelope and papers from the table, grabbed his coat and Goliath's leash from the hall, and stormed out of the house.

He *knew* that he had handed over the envelope exactly as he'd been given it.

Which meant, as far as David could

see, that Miss Gorringer had actually given him an envelope stuffed with paper.

And why should she do a thing like that?

David didn't know, but he was determined to find out.

With Goliath beside him he marched up the steps and raised his hand to knock on Miss Gorringer's front door.

Then he lowered it again.

The front door was standing ajar.

Remembering the cats, David told Goliath to "Stay!"

He went cautiously into the darkened hall.

The door that led to Miss Gorringer's apartment was closed, but it opened when he turned the handle.

David stepped inside. "Miss Gorringer!" he called. "Are you there?"

There was no reply.

David looked around the darkened room, and five pairs of cats' eyes looked back at him.

But there was no sign of Miss Gorringer.

Like the party money, she had disappeared.

Chapter Four

The Rescue

David stood looking around the empty apartment—empty that is, except for the silent, watchful cats.

Suddenly a voice from the doorway said, "Miss Gorringer, where have you . . ."

The voice broke off. David turned and saw a worried, motherly-looking woman.

"I heard someone moving and thought it must be Miss Gorringer," she said.

"I'm looking for her myself," said David. "You don't know where she is, do you?"

The woman shook her head. "I'm worried about her. I'm Mrs. Potter from the apartment upstairs. We always try to keep an eye on Miss Gorringer, but today when I dropped in to see her she'd just vanished. She's been gone for ages. The funny thing is, she was expecting me. We always have a cup of tea about this time. I was so worried I even phoned the police, but they just said to wait for a bit and call back if she doesn't turn up."

"Maybe she's just gone out shopping," said David.

The woman shook her head. "Not this late, and not for this long," she said. "She never leaves her cats alone for longer than she can help. Why on earth should she just vanish like this?"

David couldn't help thinking about the missing money. Could Miss Gorringer have run off with it? But then, that didn't make sense. A hundred dollars was a lot of money, but it wasn't really enough to tempt anyone to run off to South America. Besides, Miss Gorringer would never run away and leave her beloved cats.

Suddenly a gleam of gold beneath the sofa caught his eye. He bent down and fished out Miss Gorringer's glasses.

"She'd never have gone out without them," said Mrs. Potter, more worried than ever. "I'm sure she's fallen down or been run over."

David looked around the apartment, searching desperately for some clue. He looked at the cats. One black, one white, one black and white, one tortoiseshell, and one tabby . . .

"Where's Ginger?" he said. "Ginger's missing!"

As soon as he asked the question, David knew the answer. Ginger had run away, almost certainly to the park. Miss Gorringer had rushed out after him, leaving her glasses behind and the door open.

She must have been in a complete panic. Her coat was on the door—she hadn't even taken that.

David looked out of the window. It was getting dark now and snowing hard.

David remembered what his father had said about the danger of older people falling down . . .

If Miss Gorringer were out there in

the park, lying hurt with no one to help her . . . David remembered hearing that older people couldn't stand too much cold. She could be very ill, perhaps dead before anyone found her.

David thought of calling the police again, but there was no time to wait for them. It was up to him—and to Goliath.

He turned to Mrs. Potter. "Is there anything here she wore a lot?"

Mrs. Potter waved towards a woolen scarf. "She always wore that when she went out."

David snatched up the scarf and hurried off. His dad had often said Goliath was part bloodhound . . .

He ran down the snowy steps and waved the scarf under the nose of a puzzled Goliath. "Miss Gorringer, Goliath. Fetch!"

David didn't really expect it to work. But to his surprise Goliath sniffed hard

at the scarf and then set off for the park,
towing David behind him.

The park was looking dark and
spooky by the time they reached it. It
was quite cold now, and there was no
one around.

The darkness and the snow changed
the look of everything, and soon David
felt that Miss Gorringer's might not be
the only frozen-stiff body found in the
park. He was lost—but Goliath

seemed to know exactly where he was going.

He led David around the base of the hill to a little wooded hollow on the other side.

It was pitch black under the trees and things looked *really* scary.

Goliath whined impatiently and tugged him on.

It took all David's courage to go into the little wood. He kept expecting the trees to reach out and grab him. But he made himself go on—and in the end it was worth it.

Goliath led David straight to Miss Gorringer, who lay huddled up at the foot of a tree, a big ginger cat held tightly in her arms. "Are you all right?" called David.

She looked up at him. "Thank goodness you came David." Her voice was faint and she was shivering hard.

"Ginger ran away, and so I came to look for him. I found him, but then I slipped and sprained my ankle . . . I'm so cold and tired."

"It's all right," said David. "Goliath tracked you down. We'll soon have you home again."

He helped her to her feet, still clutching the struggling cat, and made her put her arm around his shoulders so he could help her walk.

David turned to Goliath. "Home!" he said, and Goliath led them across the rapidly darkening park and back to Miss Gorringer's apartment.

David got her to sit down and made her a nice cup of tea. He gave her her glasses back, too.

Goliath came in, too, and sat on the carpet quite peacefully, entirely surrounded by cats.

Once he was quite sure that Miss

Gorringer was more or less all right, David said, "Miss Gorringer, there's something I need to ask you, about the money for the party."

He told her what had happened, and Miss Gorringer looked puzzled. Suddenly she laughed.

"David, look inside that old cookie jar tin on the mantelpiece." David looked, and found a bundle of bills held together with a rubber band. He held it out. "Is this the party money?"

"I'm afraid so, David," said Miss Gorringer apologetically. "And you know what ought to be in there? Some knitting patterns from a magazine! I'm afraid I got into a flap about being ready for the party—I'd lost my glasses—and somehow in all the fuss I put the wrong bundle of paper in the envelope and gave it to you. I'm so sorry, David."

"That's all right," said David

cheerfully. "All's well that ends well. If you're sure you're all right for a few minutes I'll just run this money down to the restaurant. It's nearly opening time . . ."

*   *   *

The Christmas party was a huge success, and everybody had a wonderful time.

David's mom and dad came and got Miss Gorringer and took her to the emergency room of the local hospital, where they strapped up her ankle. After that Miss Gorringer insisted on being driven to the party. She sat in an armchair by the fire and watched everyone having a good time.

At the end of the party there was champagne for everyone, and Miss Gorringer insisted on giving a toast.

"Ladies and gentlemen, I give you two people who made this party possible. Without them *you* wouldn't be here now,

and *I* wouldn't be anywhere, probably not even alive. I should like you to raise your glasses to David and Goliath!"

"David and Goliath!" shouted everybody.

David went red, and Goliath barked excitedly at the sound of his name.

After the party David and Goliath went out into the street and started walking back home. His parents were driving Miss Gorringer home, but David had said he'd sooner walk.

The snow-covered street was silent, and the stars were bright and clear in the winter sky.

It was snowing again, and David heaved a sigh of pure contentment. Tomorrow was Christmas Eve, the snow hadn't melted, and it was going to be a white Christmas after all.

Somehow David knew it was going to be the best Christmas of his life.

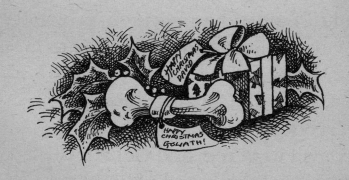